# OK WILL GET YOU TO SLEEP!

Words by
## Jory John

Pictures by
## Olivier Tallec

Farrar Straus Giroux
New York

Attention, reader.

Ahem. Let's try that again.

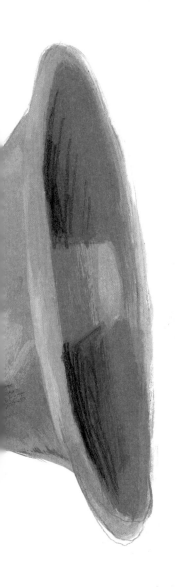

# ATTENTION, READER!!!

This book will get you to **SLEEP**.

It's **TRUE**.

By the end of it,
you'll be sleeping **PEACEFULLY**.

So get ready to **SLEEP**!

Let's all say it together:

# GETTTTTTTT READDDDDDDDDY TO SLEEEEEEEEEEEP!!!

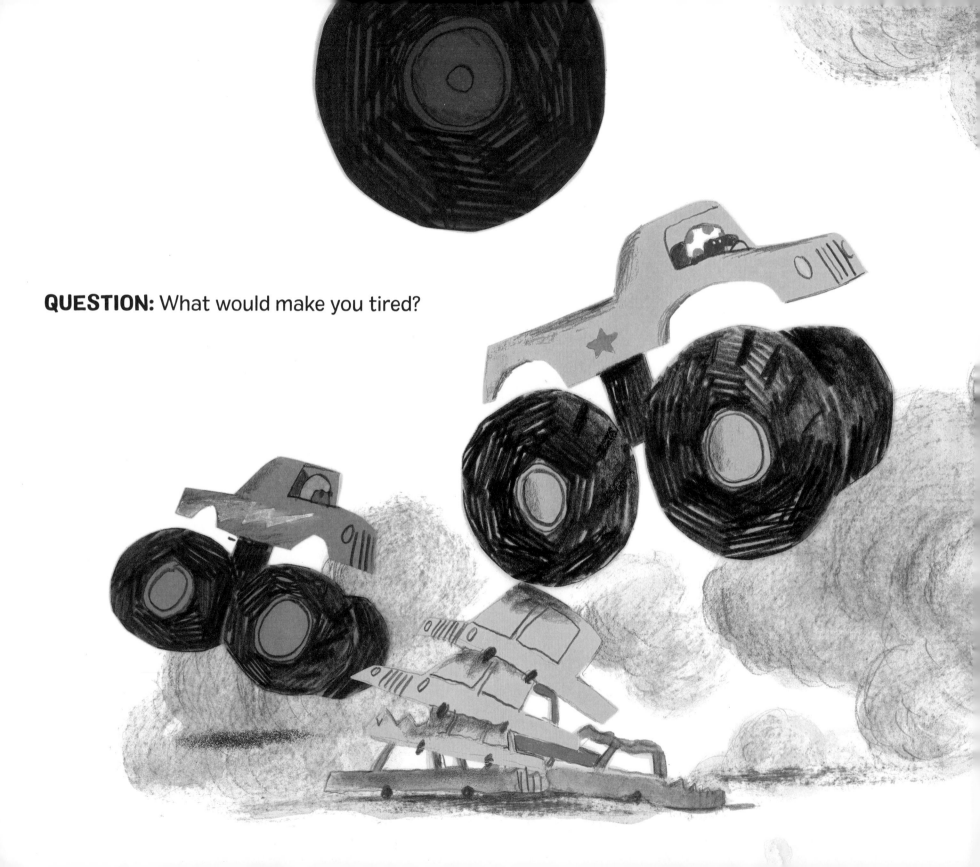

**QUESTION:** What would make you tired?

**ANSWER:** About fifty monster trucks **RUMBLING** and **BUMBLING** and **CRASHING** through these pages.

See?

**YOU TIRED YET???**

**QUESTION:** What **ELSE** would make you tired?

**ANSWER:** About fifty **ELECTRIC GUITARS** jamming out on some **WICKED, ENDLESS** guitar solos.

# RAOO RAOOO RAOOOOOOOO!!!

**YOU ASLEEP YET???**

**QUESTION:** What **ELSE** would make you tired?

**ANSWER:** About fifty **CAR ALARMS** going off simultaneously.

# MURRRRRRP! MURRRRRRP! MURRRRRRRP!

**YOU DREAMING YET???**

No? Oh. Hmm.
A bit stubborn, eh?
A really reluctant sleeper.

Maybe a chant will help.
Feel free to chant along:

FALL ASLEEP! FALL ASLEEP! FALL ASLEEP! FALL ASLEEP
FALL ASLEEP FALL ASLEEP! FALL ASLEEP FALL ASLEEP
FALL ASLEEP! FALL ASLEEP FALL ASLEEP FALL ASLEEP!

Psst! Pssssssssssssssst!
Did the chant help?
It didn't?
That's odd.
The chant usually works.

Let me think . . . Let me
think . . . Just let
me think . . .

Oh!

I've got it!

What about a magic trick??

Here goes . . .

On the count of three, you will be fast asleep. Got it?

Now, work with me here.

One . . . two . . . get ready . . . are you ready?

Don't say you're ready if you're not ready . . .

One again . . . two again . . . **THREE**!!

Snap! **YOU'RE ASLEEP**!

And the magic trick **WORKED**!!!

GOOOOOOOD NIIIIIIIIIIGHT, MAGGGGICCCC- FANNNNNN!

Hmm?
You're wide-a—*what?*
You're wide-**AWAKE**?

Well, don't fret.
Sometimes it takes longer than *other* times
to fall asleep.
And I still have **PLENTY** of tricks up the ol'
sleeve. The ol' *book* sleeve.

For instance, what if you **WOOF** yourself to sleep? Go ahead. Try it.
Repeat after me:

# WOOF WOOF WOOF! WOOF WOOF WOOF! WOOF WOOF WOOF!

Anything? Did you **WOOF** yourself to sleep? You didn't?

Well . . . how about you **MEOW**
yourself to sleep, then?
Go ahead. Try it.
Just repeat after me:

MEOW MEOW MEOW!
MEOW MEOW MEOW!
MEOW MEOW MEOW!

Sheesh!
You're really holding out.
Usually, all of this stuff works perfectly.
Usually, you'd have been fast asleep for
**HOURS** by now.

I just don't understand why you're still awake.
I didn't want to resort to this, but here goes . . .

We're pulling out the sheep.

Ah, yes, the sheep!

Counting sheep *always* works. It's the oldest trick in this book—or *any* book.

# HERE COME THE SHEEP!

Okay, sleepy reader, you're going to count every single sheep that jumps over that fence.
Got it?
Good.
Let's do this . . .
But wait. Before we start . . .
there's more . . .
because the sheep are being chased . . .

by **DRAGONS**!!!

# RARR RARR RARR!

Count the sheep **AND** the dragons!

**ARE YOU COUNTING THEM???**
**WHY ISN'T THIS WORKING?!?!?!**

Something is awry.
By now you should be
sleeping, and this book should've
worked perfectly.
Why won't you sleep? Be honest.

It's . . . *what*?
It's this *very book* that's the problem?
Well, I never!

# WELL, I NEVER!

So . . . what would help you
fall asleep, then?
Less yelling?
Fewer monster trucks?
No dragons chasing sheep?
Putting away this book?
Reading something else entirely?

But what **FUN** is **THAT**?

Sigh.

Okay, okay. I understand.

I think we have a new plan.

You'll read something less fun.

Go ahead.

No need to thank me, but you're very
welcome.

Yes, you're **VERY** welcome.

Good night.

Let's all say it together: **GOOOOOOOOOOOOOOD**

To Tessa and Doug —J.J.

Farrar Straus Giroux Books for Young Readers
An imprint of Macmillan Publishing Group, LLC
120 Broadway, New York, NY 10271
mackids.com

Our books may be purchased in bulk for promotional, educational, or business use.
Please contact your local bookseller or the Macmillan Corporate and Premium Sales Department
at (800) 221-7945 ext. 5442 or by email at MacmillanSpecialMarkets@macmillan.com.

Library of Congress Cataloging-in-Publication Data is available.

First edition, 2022
Book design by Mercedes Padró and Lisa Vega
Color separations by Bright Arts (H.K.) Ltd.
Printed in China by RR Donnelley Asia Printing Solutions Ltd.,
Dongguan City, Guangdong Province

ISBN 978-0-374-31130-8 (hardcover)
1 3 5 7 9 10 8 6 4 2